POPPY AND BIG ADVENTURE

Inspired By The True Story of Two Chincoteague Ponies

Written by
Martha C. McNiel

Illustrated by
Aleksandra Szymanska

Copyright ©2024 Martha C. McNiel

Written by Martha C. McNiel
Illustrated by Aleksandra Szymanska

Photo of Martha C. McNiel (self-photo)
Photo of Aleksandra Szymanska by Martha C. McNiel
Photos of Poppy and Daisy by Martha C. McNiel
Photo of Nick by Sam McNiel

Published by Miriam Laundry Publishing Company
miriamlaundry.com

All rights reserved. This book or any portion thereof may not be reproduced or used in any manner whatsoever without the express written permission from the author except for the use of brief quotations in a book review.

HC ISBN 978-1-77944-132-4
PB ISBN 978-1-77944-131-7
e-Book ISBN 978-1-77944-130-0

FIRST EDITION

The sun was shining warmly on the sand. Tails swished at the flies buzzing around the band of wild, sleepy ponies.

Suddenly the stallion's head jerked up as he heard pounding hoof beats in the distance. All the horses raised their heads.

"Wake up, Poppy!" her mother said quickly. "The Cowboys are coming!"

Whooping and hollering, the Saltwater Cowboys appeared from behind the dunes. They soon rounded up the wild pony mares and their late summer foals.

Several days later, Poppy and her mother Bliss were at the Chincoteague Carnival Grounds. The Saltwater Cowboys came early in the morning and started loading the foals into waiting trailers. Today, they would go to their new homes with the people who bought them in the Fall Foal Auction.

Shrill neighs broke the misty morning air as foals and their mothers called to each other.

Then, the metal door slammed shut, and the trailer began to move.

"What's happening?" Poppy exclaimed. "I'm scared!"

A brown and white foal standing next to her said softly, "Me too!"

"I'm Poppy. What's your name?"

"Daisy," replied the pretty pinto.

For several hours, the trailer hummed and bounced as the tires rolled under the ponies' feet. Then, all of a sudden, the trailer was still and quiet.

Poppy wondered, *What is going to happen now?*

The trailer door opened slowly.

"Where are we?" Poppy asked.

"I have no idea!" Daisy replied.

Peeking out the open door, the foals hopped down onto the cold ground and looked around.

A woman said, "Welcome to Pony Kindergarten!"

Poppy and Daisy soon found out that they had arrived at Stoney Creek Chincoteagues in Hughesville, Pennsylvania. Stoney Creek is a famous farm that helps wild ponies learn how to get along in the world of humans.

Pony Kindergarten was a lot of fun! The baby ponies learned to eat new foods and to wear a halter. They made friends and played with giant balls.

They learned that people offer scratches that feel good, and if you follow the feed pan, the humans will let you have a tasty bite of sweet grain.

The foals got vaccinations to stay healthy, and they got their first hoof trims! There was so much to learn that the ponies didn't have time to feel sad or scared for very long. The wild seashores and salty air of Assateague Island now seemed very far away.

After eight weeks in Pony Kindergarten, it was Graduation Day!

That night, even though it was snowing, a horse trailer pulled up to the barn. It was time to go. Pretending to be brave, Poppy and Daisy walked up the ramp into the big, dark trailer.

"Goodbye, Poppy! Goodbye, Daisy!" the other ponies called.

"I'll miss you all!" Poppy cried softly.

Daisy gave her friend a big hug.

In the trailer Poppy and Daisy shared a big stall filled with soft shavings and lots of hay.

After four days traveling across the United States, the trailer finally stopped in California. The doors opened and a kind man and woman came into the trailer. The woman said, "Hi Daisy! Hi Poppy! Welcome to DreamPower Horsemanship!"

20

The man attached lead ropes to their halters and led the ponies out into the bright sunshine. Poppy and Daisy saw horses looking at them as they walked into their new barn. "I wonder if they are friendly?" Poppy whispered to Daisy.

"I hope so!" Daisy whispered back.

Poppy and Daisy ate fresh hay, took long drinks of fresh water, and took a look around. In the stall next door was an older mare named Honey.

"Can you tell me where we are?" Poppy asked her.

At first, Honey seemed annoyed. She didn't have much time for silly young ponies.

After some grumbling, she said, "DreamPower is a special farm where horses and humans become friends. We help children and adults feel happier and not so afraid."

"How do we do that?" Daisy asked.

Honey thought for a moment. "We show them how to become friends with horses. While doing that, they also learn how to be better friends with humans and how to be kind."

Six months later, the warm July sun was beating down. Poppy and Daisy were standing in the shade of the barn, tails quietly swishing at the flies buzzing around the sleepy ponies.

"Who's that?" Poppy said, lifting her head as voices sounded in the barn aisle.

Honey answered. "That's one of the therapists who works here. Looks like she has a new client."

A young girl and a woman walked towards them.

"Anna, these are the newest ponies at DreamPower," the therapist said. "Would you like to meet them?"

Anna looked at her therapist and then at the ground. She let out a big sigh. Daisy's kind eyes watched as she stopped at the stall door.

Poppy walked forward to say hello.
Anna slowly reached out her hand.
"She's so soft!" Anna smiled.

Poppy leaned into Anna's hand for more scratches.

Anna's eyes filled with tears as she stroked Poppy's neck. Poppy blew out a soft sigh as Anna gave her a quiet hug.

It had been a very long journey for Poppy and Daisy. Now they knew that their real home was DreamPower, and that their big adventure was just beginning.

IMPORTANT WORDS

Assateague Island — A barrier island located off the eastern coast of Virginia and Maryland, USA.

Chincoteague Pony — The Chincoteague Pony is from Assateague Island. The Virginia herd of Chincoteague Ponies is owned by the Chincoteague Volunteer Fire Company.

Chincoteague Volunteer Fire Company — Organized in 1924 on Chincoteague Island, Virginia, the CVFC is now one of the most successful and modern volunteer fire companies on the East Coast, USA.

DreamPower Horsemanship — A nonprofit therapeutic horsemanship program located in Gilroy, California.

Foal — A young horse or pony up to one year old.

Halter — A leather or nylon headgear for a horse or pony.

Mare — An adult female horse or pony.

Pinto — A horse or pony with a dark background coloring and random patches of white.

Saltwater Cowboys — Members of the Chincoteague Volunteer Fire Company who take care of the Chincoteague Pony herd in Virginia.

Stallion — An adult male horse or pony.

Stoney Creek Chincoteagues — A famous farm in Hughesville, Pennsylvania that specializes in training young wild ponies.

Vaccination - An effective way to protect horses and ponies from harmful diseases.

Made in the USA
Monee, IL
01 July 2025